The illustrations in this book are drawn by hand on a graphics tablet and are finished using natural colour palettes and textures.

First published in the Czech Republic as *Gerda Příběh velryby* in 2018 by Albatros Media a.s. First published in English by
Floris Books in 2019. Illustrations and story © 2018 Adrián Macho. Original Czech text by Peter Kavecký
English version © 2019 Floris Books. All rights reserved. No part of this book may be reproduced
without the prior permission of Floris Books, Edinburgh www.florisbooks.co.uk
British Library CIP Data available. ISBN 978-178250-559-4. Printed in China by Imago

The Whale

the Sea and the Stars

Adrián Macho

Floris Books

In a blue, blue ocean, as wide and deep as you can imagine,
there lived a little whale named Gerda. She had a mother,
a father, and a brother called Lars. Gerda was happy leaping
and splashing with Lars, and she also loved swimming close
to her mother.

When Lars grew bigger, he set off on his own to swim the
world's oceans and find a good life for himself.

Gerda's mother told her that one day she would leave too.
Every night, she sang an old whale song:

Little one, you are born of the stars and the sea,
Your life will be long and full, my love,
As you swim the world's oceans, happy and free,
The sea will curve round you, the stars shine above.

Travel the world as you learn, as you grow,
Explore all the shallows and deeps, my sweet,
Life is a journey and soon you will go,
You have shores to discover and creatures to meet.

On some waves we're cradled, on some we are tossed,
But, little one, they are yours to ride,
If you are doubtful or if you are lost,
Stars still shine over you: they'll be your guide.

One day, little one, you will see a new place,
Somewhere so sparkling, you'll no longer roam,
We all want adventures, then need a safe base,
Trust your heart: it will sing when you find your true home.

The time came for Gerda to set off on her own, carrying her mother's song in her heart.

She let the current take her a long, long way south, where the water grew much colder. She spotted penguins floating on a chunk of ice. *Splish!* One penguin flopped forwards into the water. *Splish!* Another one followed. They wriggled back onto the ice and flopped again.

Splish! Wriggle. *Splish!* Wriggle.

"Eee-ee-ee," called Gerda, which means 'Hello' in whale language. "Can I play?"

"Nooooo, hee hee hee," laughed the penguins. "We're learning to plunge deep to catch fish. You're too huge to leap and plunge!"

But Gerda leapt all the time with her brother Lars. With a wave of her big tail, she surged out of the waves and landed on the ice. Laughing, she slipped back – *ker-sploshhh!* – into the sea.

The penguins stopped to watch. "She's huge, but she *can* play!" they squealed.

Gerda had fun with the penguins for a while, then she remembered her mother's song:

Explore all the shallows and deeps, my sweet.

She swam north and dived down to the ocean floor, where she found a grouchy octopus. He was guarding a pile of sunken garbage, muttering to himself. He picked up an old pot, then dropped it so he could grab a bottle. Then he dropped that and snatched a tyre.

"Eee-ee-ee," Gerda said politely.

"What do you want, bothersome young whale?" grumped the octopus. "Can't you see I'm busy? So much treasure, and only eight tentacles to hold it with!"

"You must sometimes wish for twelve tentacles!" replied Gerda.

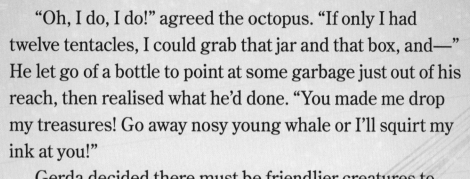

"Oh, I do, I do!" agreed the octopus. "If only I had twelve tentacles, I could grab that jar and that box, and—" He let go of a bottle to point at some garbage just out of his reach, then realised what he'd done. "You made me drop my treasures! Go away nosy young whale or I'll squirt my ink at you!"

Gerda decided there must be friendlier creatures to talk with, and she swam on.

Gerda drew close to the coast, where she could see a lighthouse and green rolling hills. She hummed her mother's song:

You have shores to discover and creatures to meet.

The gulls were chattering. "Oh-oh-oh-oh-oh," they cawed. Seagulls make their nests on land, thought Gerda, even though they can sleep on the water. They must know everything! I will learn so much from them!

"Did you know…?" cawed the gulls loudly. "Have you heard…? You'll never guess… Oh-oh-oh-oh-oh."

"Eee-ee-ee," called Gerda.

"Eee-ee-ee yourself," replied the gulls. "What do you think…? Oooh, I tell you what…"

Gerda listened a while longer, and the gulls gossipped on and on, but didn't say much about the shore, or about anything else. At least they're chattier than the octopus! she said to herself, and went on her way.

Gerda had travelled a great distance. She loved exploring, but her heart began to long for something more. She thought of her mother's song:

We all want adventures, then need a safe base.

When will I stop travelling? she wondered. I've felt the cold of the south, I've seen the bottom of the sea, I've swum along the shore. Where is my place?

While she was thinking, a couple of sharp-toothed killer whales glided close.

"Eee-ee-ee," Gerda said nervously. "Hello killer whales."

"Eee-ee-ee," they replied. "You know, we're not *actually* whales at all, we're big dolphins. We prefer to be called orcas."

"OK! Hello orcas," said Gerda more confidently. "I'm Gerda, and I *am* a whale. I've been on a long journey, but now I'm ready to find my own special place. Only, I'm not sure where to look."

"Hmmm, that's tricky," said the biggest orca. "Why don't you ask the wise narwhal of the north pole? He knows everything."

"I haven't been to the north pole yet." Gerda felt more hopeful. "Thank you, orcas!"

As Gerda swam north, the water grew cold once more.

"Hello whale," said a voice.

She turned to see a thoughtful polar bear, gazing at the sky. "Eee-ee-ee," she replied.

"Where are you travelling to?" asked the bear.

"I've come to find the wise narwhal," said Gerda. "Why are you looking at the stars?"

"I am talking to the Star Bear," the polar bear replied. "When I have a question, that's who I ask. She twinkles, and then I know what's best."

"Oh, I didn't know bears could be made of stars." Gerda gazed upwards. She remembered her mother's song:

If you are doubtful or if you are lost,
Stars still shine over you: they'll be your guide.

"Stars are very helpful," said the polar bear. "To find your narwhal, you should follow the North Star."

"Oh, thank you, polar bear!" called Gerda, and her heart lifted.

Gerda followed the North Star. When it was high above her, she knew she was at the north pole, and she dived down down down and discovered a shimmering underwater ice cave.

"Welcome, young whale," said a soft, calm voice. It was the narwhal himself. He was a whale with a wonderful tusk on his head. "Why are you here?" he asked.

"I need your help, wise narwhal," blurted Gerda, forgetting to say hello.

"We all need help sometimes," said the narwhal.

"I have been on a long journey," said Gerda. "I have seen the far cold south, the ocean depths, the long shores and the icy north. I've met many creatures, but now I want to stop travelling and find a special place of my own. How will I know when my journey is finished?" Her question came pouring out.

"Your exploring has made you stronger than you realise, young whale," said the narwhal. "Let me think..."

Gerda waited patiently while the wise narwhal pondered. Eventually he said, "If you swim to warmer waters, then east, you may find happiness. Follow the stars and follow your heart, and you will know when your journey is at its end."

"Oh, thank you, narwhal," said Gerda.

"Good luck, young whale," replied the narwhal. Then he went on slowly, "I have met many creatures, and I have heard many questions. But a while ago I met a young whale very like you, with a question like yours too."

"Oh!" Gerda said. "Do you know where that young whale went?"

"I told him what I've told you," said the wise narwhal. Gerda set off again following the narwhal's directions.

She was glad it was night and she could see the stars reflected in the water, but she was so tired. She had come such a long way. She drifted in the currents, and sang to herself:

Little one, you are born of the stars and the sea,
Your life will be long and full, my love,
As you swim the world's oceans, happy and free,
The sea will curve round you, the stars shine above.

Dreamily she wondered whether
someone was singing her song
back to her.

Someone *was* singing the song back to her. Gerda opened her eyes wide: there, in a beautiful starlit bay, was her brother: Lars!

"Lars! Lars! Eee-ee-ee!" she called.

"Gerda! Gerda! Eee-ee-ee!" he called back.

They leapt in swirls and splashes, and they talked all night about the playful, grumpy, gossipy creatures they had met on their travels. Gerda told her brother, "The wise narwhal said he had met another young whale."

"That was me!" Lars was amazed. "But Gerda, wait until morning comes, you won't believe what you see here."

As the sun rose, it lit up the most beautiful bay Gerda had come across in her long journey through the world's oceans.

She saw more and more whales: Beluga whales and
grey whales, beaked whales and bowhead whales,
humpback whales and right whales, all living happily
among creatures of the shallows and deeps.

Gerda's heart sang, and she knew her journey was over.

Her mother's words ran through her thoughts:

This place is so sparkling, I'll no longer roam,
My heart sings because I have found my true home.

This book is the property of.
Leven. Art. for Pleasure Group.

This book is the property of.
Leven. Art. for Pleasure Group.